100%
Meditation

100% Meditation

By Sirshree Tejparkhi

Copyright © Tejgyan Global Foundation
All Rights Reserved 2017

Tejgyan Global Foundation is a charitable organization
with its headquarters in Pune, India.

Published by WOW Publishings Pvt. Ltd., India

First edition published in January 2017

Second reprint in November 2018

Copyrights are reserved with Tejgyan Global Foundation and publishing rights are vested exclusively with WOW Publishings Pvt. Ltd. This book is sold subject to the condition that it shall not by way of trade or otherwise, be lent, resold, hired out, or otherwise circulated without the publisher's prior written consent in any form of binding or cover other than that in which it is published and without a similar condition including this condition being imposed on the subsequent purchaser and without limiting the rights under copyright reserved above, no part of this publication may be reproduced, stored in or introduced into a retrieval system, or transmitted, in any form, or by any means, electronic, mechanical, photocopying, recording or otherwise, without the prior written permission of both the copyright owner and the above-mentioned publisher of this book. Any person who does any unauthorized act in relation to this publication may be liable to criminal prosecution and civil claims for damages.

Table of Contents

	Introduction	1
1.	What is Meditation	3
2.	Benefits of Meditation	9
3.	Common Myths about Meditation	20
4.	Distractions to Self-meditation	29
5.	Roadblocks in Meditation	33
6.	Preparing for Meditation	44
7.	The Art of Witnessing	51
8.	Sense of Being	63
9.	The Thoughtless State	68
10.	The Path and the Ultimate Goal	73

Introduction

We all seek love, peace and joy in life. In every pursuit that we undertake in life, our real yearning is for experiencing lasting love, unshakeable peace and joy. We have an innate tendency to look for joy that cannot diminish. In pursuit of this, we strive hard to achieve whatever can bring us these.

It may seem to be difficult to find it within us, but it is impossible to find it outside in the material world. The clear understanding of true meditation and its consistent practice can lead us to the fulfillment of this innate need for completeness.

The word meditation has been confined to techniques, rituals, process or exercise. Truly speaking, the essence of meditation is not in techniques, but in clearly realizing the nature of who-we-truly-are. The practice of meditation with right understanding leads us to transcend the tendencies of the mind and stabilize in our true nature of pure consciousness.

This book is like the Ocean in a drop. It is part of the 'Ocean in a Drop' series. It brings a deep understanding of meditation through a series of question and answers between seekers and Sirshree.

These conversations will help you discover the real meaning of meditation. It will bring about a paradigm shift in the understanding of what meditation is and what makes it 100%.

Scattered in these answers are 100 precious drops 💧, which have been annotated for repeated reading. Reading these profound drops of wisdom and contemplating upon them can bring about a transformation in the way we approach meditation and its real purpose.

1

What is Meditation

Seeker 1: I have been practicing meditation and have some questions. My friends, too, have been practicing meditation. But, when I hear them discussing about meditation and its results, I really wonder whether I am on the right path. Please guide me on how I can progress in this practice of meditation.

Sirshree: Sure. Before that, what does meditation mean for you?

Seeker 1: I've read and seen pictures of yogis sitting with closed eyes for long hours in meditation. I understand that it is an exercise of concentration for the mind. I've heard that meditation helps in gaining control over our thoughts.

Sirshree: Ok. Good. What do others think?

Seeker 2: For me, meditation means renouncing worldly life. I visualize a hermit sitting in the Himalayas for long hours with closed eyes.

Seeker 3: I consider meditation as an exercise to gain control over thoughts and emotions.

Sirshree: Very good. But these are just few benefits of meditation. Let's consider what meditation essentially is.

(1) *Meditation is essentially an attribute of the Ultimate Witnessor, the real experiencer of all experiences. This witnessor is also called God, Allah, Self, Self-Awareness, or Consciousness.* It is that source within us which is awake even in deep sleep; it is self-awareness, which is present even in the state of non-awareness.

(2) *Meditation is our true nature, inseparable from who-we-truly-are.* The real essence of meditation is the state of beingness; a state that exists beyond thoughts. *This state of beingness is who-we-truly-are. In other words, we are meditation*, though this may sound strange at first. Meditation is the experience of the real Self. We will talk about this in detail.

Seeker 2: Isn't meditation actually the religious practice of Hinduism? I've rarely known meditation being referred in the tenets of other religions.

Sirshree: Many people link mediation to religious beliefs. But in fact, meditation is our true essence and is beyond religious beliefs. (3) *It is our actual religion. Just being a Hindu, Muslim, Sikh, Christian or Jew is not religion. To know our true nature and abide in it, is true religion.* Meditation is our nature, our basic disposition. The true meaning of religion is our basic innate nature.

Sufis meditate out of devotion for the Creator through their whirling practice. Jesus has expounded the practice of meditation as being in communion with the Father – the Source of everything. So meditation is not just a practice of a particular sect of people.

It is the wealth that raises human consciousness. Meditation enables you to take the right decisions in life and to be always happy, while also radiating joy to others. Having attained the wealth of true meditation, one never loses his level of consciousness.

Seeker 2: This is wonderful. So what I have understood as meditation is not true meditation.

Sirshree: There is one more very important understanding about meditation. The simple meaning of meditation is 'doing nothing'.

Seeker 2: Sirshree, how can we do nothing? Doing nothing is so difficult, as much as sitting in meditation.

Sirshree: The simple meaning of meditation is 'doing nothing'. As you rightly said, for many people, 'doing nothing' becomes very difficult. A man was displeased because his son was doing nothing. One fine day, the lad joins a meditation course. Now the father is very pleased and brags, "Now, my son, together with many other people, is really doing 'nothing'."

How to do nothing? It is like asking, "What should be done to get sleep?" "You have to do 'nothing' to get sleep, just go and lie down. If you are trying to get sleep through effort, sleep will elude you. Otherwise, you can get sleep without doing anything easily." In the same way, meditation is a process in which there is no need to do anything; you only have to be. You should do nothing and also not try to do nothing – even trying to do nothing amounts to doing something! *Meditation leads you to the state of awareness beyond 'doing' and 'non-doing'.*

Seeker 2: So is doing nothing the ultimate aim of meditation?

Sirshree: *Meditation is a path; meditation on the Self is the destination.*

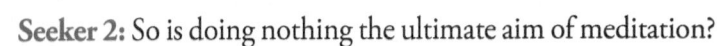

The techniques designed to begin meditation or to improve concentration have also been popularly known as 'meditation'. These so-called 'meditations' or concentration practices are a path to Self-Meditation. *Self-Meditation means being absorbed in the 'Self' – the formless space-less universal consciousness, which is present everywhere – within and outside, and also beyond both! This is the real aim of meditation.*

Therefore, the word 'Self-Meditation' can be considered more appropriate than the word 'meditation.' Just improving concentration is not the goal of meditation. Concentration is a ladder in the path of meditation. Concentration improves with meditation. But if someone is meditating with the aim of improving concentration, then he is taking the least benefit of meditation. He has mistaken the means to be the end.

Many a time, it so happens that one begins on the path of meditation to attain realization of the true Self, but becomes satisfied with improved concentration or by gaining some mystical powers. As a result, he strays away from his real goal. He wrongly believes such gains to be the goal.

Seeker 3: Why has meditation been given so much importance?

Sirshree: Awareness is the essence of meditation. Awareness is necessary in every field of life, so much, so that no work can be done without awareness. The body receives the vital drive for action from awareness. Hence, meditation, which is the practice of raising awareness, has been given a lot of importance.

The triggers for all our activities are the five senses of our body – the senses of sight, sound, smell, taste and touch. By senses, we don't mean the organs of perception like the eyes or ears, but rather their power of perception. For example, the eye is not the sense, but the power of sight possessed by the eye is the real sense. So all five senses affect our body in one way or the other. Usually, when our senses are directed outward, they get involved in external objects and all energy gets invested in the external content of the senses. Therefore, it is necessary that we have some control over our senses. *Meditation makes it possible to internalize our attention, which was being consumed in externalized focus. It shifts the attention from external perceptions and helps to be absorbed within on that which enables you to perceive. This is true meditation.*

Seeker 1: From what I understand, meditation is required to help control the mind and senses.

Sirshree: The real purpose of meditation is to abide in Self-awareness. Let's understand this further. Our mind cannot remain idle. It incessantly demands more and more activity. As a result, we end up assigning it work that is actually unnecessary. When the mind is idle, it tends to indulge in comparing, judging, labeling, fixating, finding faults, or engaging in conflicts. This happens so subtly, that it cannot be clearly noticed without higher awareness. If there is no food for the mind in the present moment, it can dig into the past. It can grieve, repent or resent past incidents. If it is not in the past, the mind may be drawn into the future and perhaps become anxious. In this way, it never remains in the present. The mind constantly vacillates between past and future. Although both – remembering the past and considering the future – are important, this is only to the extent that actually helps us deal with the present.

Seeker 1: Yes. At times these thoughts of past and future actually drain my energy, making it difficult for me to work any further.

Sirshree: That's what a restless mind does. It drains your energy. In such situations, you may find yourself stressed and agitated. The more you try to control your mind, the more it rebels and retaliates. But the more you obey it, the more it dominates you. You may try to escape the mind's clutches by indulging in entertainment or pursuing hobbies, but the mind bounces back to regain control.

As the mind saps our creative energy, we find it difficult to focus on the work at hand leading to decline in our productivity. As a result, we cannot fulfill the expectations set by the mind and our anxiety and stress level. This adversely affects relationships at home and the workplace. One loses confidence, which often leads to depression.

Every time impurities – such as boredom, egoism, discrimination, fear, anger, greed, jealousy or hatred – arise, you experience a lack of inner freedom.

Once you are established in the experience of Self-awareness – in who-you-truly-are – the world outside will not affect you. This in turn will help in raising your productivity.

2

Benefits of Meditation

Seeker 1: Meditation can help in calming the mind and raising our productivity. These are great incentives to practice meditation. Are there any other benefits?

Sirshree: Although calmness and productivity are visible benefits of meditation, there are many deeper benefits of meditation that help us in the inner world within us.

Seeker 1: I would like to understand both these benefits. This will keep me motivated to inculcate the habit of practicing meditation regularly and consistently.

Sirshree: Yes. Effective decision-making is one such well-known benefit of meditation that helps in the external world. Further, meditation helps in breaking the attachment one has with thoughts and the body. As the attachment breaks, your sensitivity increases. You begin to have better control over your feelings and emotions, your awareness and energy levels increase, which lead to improved capacity to work and perform better. In other words your productivity increases. Your body and mind become more relaxed, stress-free and your health is restored. As the practice deepens, you are able to experience the joy of silence. These are some of the benefits in the external world. With consistent practice you then begin to realize the deeper benefits of meditation, which we shall discuss.

Seeker 2: I often find it difficult to control my anger; I feel consumed by situations that disappoint me. I try to suppress my feelings; at times when it becomes difficult to handle them and I blast out. You mentioned that meditation can help me have better control over feelings and emotions. So I wanted to understand how I can practice that.

Sirshree: *Meditation makes it possible for you to witness your feelings and emotions in a detached manner.* This is a deeper benefit that comes with consistent practice. Let me help you understand this. Generally, when you sense a negative or uncomfortable feeling, what do you do? You try to divert your focus by indulging in some or the other activity. You may watch TV, or dine out, go shopping, or simply vent your anger on somebody. These are nothing but distractions that divert your attention to something else so that you escape or avoid that uncomfortable feeling or emotion. But these distractions do more harm than good, and also have a negative impact on your health.

Let me give you an example: Suppose that you have had a bad day at work and are angry or upset about something. You may try to suppress your emotions by diverting your attention by walking straight to the kitchen. You start searching for something to munch or eat. You switch on the TV and keep switching channels. Now your bad feeling begins to subside. In this way, every time you suppress the emotion, you end up in the kitchen or the office pantry. You might never realize when emotional eating becomes an addiction. But eventually you know that it has had an adverse effect on your health. Not just that, but suppressed emotions also cause perturbations in the body cells, also affecting DNA. These are the seeds of disease. This is also being evidenced through scientific research around the world.

Seeker 2: Is that the reason why people with emotional stress suffer from disease and obesity?

Sirshree: Of course, difficulty in managing emotions can lead to numerous psychosomatic ailments. Most people deal with negative emotions either by suppressing them within, or expressing them by shouting aloud or abusing other people. Shouting at others will only serve the ego. It does not remove the emotional stress. You still suffer the turmoil of your emotions within. From morning to night, your emotions undergo so many changes. Whenever your mood changes or you recall old memories from the past, you give an opportunity for emotions such as grief, despair, or anguish to arise. Both your inherited genes and your childhood upbringing are a stimulus for this.

With the practice of meditation, you learn to witness such emotions as they arise in your body. You just observe them, as if they were never a part of you. They have simply arisen in the body-mind mechanism that you use. This way, you neither keep emotions within yourself nor vent them out on others. You remain detached from those emotions and their associated thoughts as they arise and drop.

Imagine you are cutting a piece of thick cloth with scissors, and you hear the scissors complain: "This cloth is so thick... It's so hard to cut... Why make cloth that is so difficult to cut?"

Here you will understand that these are the feelings of the tool you are using i.e. the scissors in this example, and are not your own. In the same way, you can observe emotions arising in your own body from the perspective of a detached witness. When you believe yourself to be the body-mind mechanism, you identify yourself with all that affects it and get overtly attached to it. But as a detached witness, you can tell yourself, "These emotions are not with me, they are not happening to who-I-truly-am. They have arisen in this tool that I use, the body–mind mechanism." The real "I", or Consciousness, is the knower of this mechanism. You witness these emotions with the recognition that they are just a temporary occurrence in the body-mind mechanism.

So you begin to witness or observe these emotions from your original state of being, that you actually are. Just like the weather changes over time, you watch your emotions change with time too. Slowly, with consistent practice of witnessing these emotions, you will see that they naturally subside and have no effect on you.

With consistent observation, your entire stock of suppressed emotions will begin to arise to the surface and disappear. You will realize that you are not this body; that it is only an instrument meant for your expression. Once you recognize that you are not the body, not just intellectually, but through direct experience, then you are no longer affected by its emotional distress. Thus, through the practice of meditation, one can be freed from all such suffering.

Seeker 3: This means that meditation has a direct impact on our body.

Sirshree: Yes. In fact, patients are regularly recommended to take rest along with their treatment or therapy. But very few people really know how to rest and relax. Most people assume relaxation to be the diversion of focus onto some pleasurable activity. *By practicing meditation, we learn the art of effortless relaxation, which promotes the restoration to health. Complete health is not just associated with the physical health of the body, but the complete wellbeing in the physical, mental, financial, social and spiritual facets of life.*

Meditation revitalizes us physically as well as mentally. We become a powerful magnet whose power attracts only positive energy. Without meditation, those entangled in negative attitudes not only repel positivity but also invite ill-health, pain, sorrow, and many other troubles upon themselves. As we go deeper into meditation, mental illnesses, such as anxiety, depression, stress, and mood swings can vanish. Diseases such as asthma, high or low blood pressure, paralysis, and heart disease have been noted to improve with the practice of meditation. Meditation has proven positive effects on the overall condition of our health, even though this is not its only goal.

Seeker 3: That's really motivating. But I have one more question associated with feelings and emotions. I feel really bad when people do not acknowledge my work or do not even thank me when I go out of the way to help them. How can meditation help me?

Sirshree: This is because you get attached to the work and expect fixed results for the action or work. With the practice of meditation, you will be able to perform all your actions with detached enthusiasm.

Let me give you an example. Many people become trapped by

the expectation of receiving rewards for their actions. Even while rendering selfless service, they may initially serve well but when their actions bear fruit, they wish to claim the credit. There is no harm in expecting credit. But that joy will be temporary and attached to the result. The practice of meditation will shift the basis for fulfilment from external preconditions to the inner experience of who-you-truly-are. As you revel in the experience of silence within, external consequences will not prevent you from experiencing true and lasting joy. So to avoid such preoccupation, and stabilize in that inner peace and bliss, you should be enthusiastic in your action, but remain detached from the fruits of your action. With consistent practice, you will gain the power to achieve this balance. You will be able to develop an attitude of detached enthusiasm. It will encourage you to perform actions enthusiastically without being attached to their results.

Further, *when you are detached from the desire to know the result of your actions, you will no longer be concerned with trivial matters like not receiving thanks in return for a compliment, or an acknowledgement for providing help.* With faith in the natural process that whatever is yours will come to you, and that nothing can stop this, you can live your daily life with a feeling of ease, assurance and acceptance.

Now consider all your activities from morning to night and contemplate "How will my life be if I perform every action with detached enthusiasm? How will I get up in the morning? How will I have food? How will I conduct my work? How will I offer help?"

Seeker 3: I can imagine how peaceful my life will be with this. As soon as we start observing the thoughts they dissolve, as if they were never there! But is there a way that we are always in this state.

Sirshree: Meditation offers the bliss of silence. By practicing meditation and observing emotions and thoughts, you begin to experience the bliss of silence. However, to be in this state of blissful silence, one needs to have the proper attitude towards meditation. If you meditate with the expectation of a blissful experience, your active mind will be constantly checking whether it's experiencing bliss. This constant checking will prevent you from going deeper into meditation. However, if you meditate quietly, without any expectations or looking out for an imagined state, you will gradually enter the deep experience of stillness. You will then realize that you can sit in that blissful state of silence for hours.

When you begin observing everything from that state, you will understand that no feeling or thought can touch or bother you, unless you choose to let it bother you. You witness everything arising from silence and dissolving into it – just like the waves in an ocean.

Seeker 2: What is the role of the mind in meditation?

Sirshree: When you are meditating, you are in the present. When you are in the present, you observe your breathing, your listening, your eyes perceiving, and perhaps your hands at some work. You are aware of everything happening in the present.

The mind has a role to play only when it dwells in the past or future. It gets worried or upset about the past or anxious about the future. The practice of meditation helps you in such situations in your daily life. If you wish to learn a valuable lesson from the past, you quickly visit your past without getting stuck in past memories. If you need to plan or contemplate something for the future, you quickly visit the future. You decide exactly where you want to go in the future. As soon as the purpose is served, you return to the present. *As soon as you are in the present, the mind surrenders and only silence prevails.*

Seeker 2: So when we are in the present, will it automatically help us become more aware of the things around us?

Sirshree: Meditation helps raise your awareness. People who consistently practice meditation and contemplate deeply are able to maintain high levels of awareness. After practicing meditation, some people claim that they can experience a clear sense of presence i.e. consciousness, while others may say that the experience is not so clear. Let me help you understand this difference with an example. If you turn on your television in the morning and open all windows and curtains, will you be able to see the television screen clearly in the daylight that streams in through the windows? No, the screen will appear pale and the colours weak and faded. Does this mean there is a problem with the television set? No, because you can view the same television screen clearly at night. Although the screen remains the same, its clarity depends on external factors.

The important point is that *the experience of Being never changes; it is only how aware you are of Being that changes.* Awareness levels may fluctuate, particularly if you don't contemplate and meditate regularly and hence it is said that those who meditate are able to maintain the higher level of awareness.

Seeker 3: I am sure this will help us be in the present and become more aware. But I also wanted to share that I tend to often indulge in daydreaming and imagining things that have never happened. This not only brings sorrow but also wastes a lot of time. How can I overcome this?

Sirshree: *Meditation helps reveal the antiques of the mind in the light of the sense of being.* It's a normal tendency of the mind to venture into an imaginary world. The mind unknowingly makes up many stories by engaging in imagined thoughts. While making up such stories, you are usually unconscious that this thought process is actually at work. As we discussed earlier, the practice of meditation helps in raising your awareness. You begin to awaken and understand the hidden dark alleys of the mind. The secrets of the mind that were in the dark begin unravelling in the light of awareness.

During meditation, ask a few questions, like: "What's going on within me? Which thoughts keep arising within me? Which stories am I weaving now?" you can witness negative thoughts that you may be holding against others, such as, "This person ignores my importance... does not respect me... is unfair... is ungrateful."

At this point, you will then guide your mind to stop pondering these thoughts. You will tell your mind firmly, "You are unaware of the complete picture and are focused on just a narrow subjective view. Come out of this imaginary world and stop weaving tales. The truth can be so vast and profound that you yet to know." With this, the mind will gradually become quieter. Your tangled thoughts will begin to untangle. You will then restore the perspective of your innate untroubled nature, leading you to your happy natural state.

Seeker 3: This is a revelation! But then how can we experience that innate untroubled nature for long when this chain of thoughts is unending?

Sirshree: Meditation brings awareness of who-you-truly-are, your original state of being. One gets caught in one's own web of misconceptions and false patterns of thought due to ignorance of one's true nature. This leads to an unconscious life steeped in sorrow and constant churning of negative imaginations. The only way out is to awaken from this slumber. When you awaken from this unconscious state and realize your true nature as pure untouched beingness, it is a eureka!

The most important question in spirituality is "Who am I?" When you delve deeper into meditation, you know this answer through your direct experience. You become aware of your sense of being; you experience who-you-truly-are. When you repeatedly ask "Who am I?" this thought begins to preside over any other thought. Thus, if something frightens you, you ask, "Who exactly is frightened?" The instant answer comes, "I am." But when you ask further "Who is this I?" you will know that your true presence is independent of fear. Fear is just arising and subsiding as a temporary occurrence in the body-mind mechanism.

By placing such constant self-enquiry upon every thought, you will discover that who-you-truly-are is indeed never bothered by worry, sorrow, or pain. This does not mean that you won't have positive feelings. Feelings of real joy, love, compassion and creative expression will automatically blossom from your true nature. *Through consistent practice of meditation, you will realize that who-you-truly-are is love, bliss and peace in essence.* Among all living beings, the unique experience of Self-realization can happen only through the human body-mind. This is the whole and sole purpose of human existence. The separate individuality, which is merely an idea of a personalized 'I', is surrendered. The body-mind mechanism then serves as a mirror for the Self – the universal 'I' – to experience and express itself. This is true devotion. Devotion is not apart from meditation. It is an integral essence of being in meditation.

Initially, the beginner is motivated to practice meditation for the sake of tangible benefits and for relief from the trials that occur in life. However, when one tastes the sweet nectar of devotion, one is prepared to surrender the personalized 'I' and abide unconditionally in the experience of nothingness. In the process, many benefits are incurred. However, the devotee is disinterested in these benefits as devotion in itself becomes the highest source of bliss and fulfilment!

3

Common Myths about Meditation

Seeker 1: I always have this feeling that meditation is difficult to practice. I struggle a lot to sit in meditation and hence tend to conclude that it's a waste of time.

Sirshree: Some people believe that meditation is very difficult and complicated. But this is just a misconception. There are practitioners who have created many of their own wrong beliefs and notions about meditation due to which many people find it difficult. When a person hears such words, he creates his own mental pictures and imaginary stories about meditation. The mind creates ideas around what has been heard, seen, read or thought about. If you ask different people about meditation, perhaps their ideas might vary. But it is *important to understand that meditation is neither difficult nor arduous. In fact, true meditation helps in cleaning the grime of such false notions and misconceptions. You are freed from such limiting beliefs and abide in pure consciousness.*

Do you consider taking a shower every day to be a waste of time? Surely not. So it is with meditation. Consider meditation as a shower you take to cleanse your mind. It's like watering a plant every day so that it grows into a big tree. It is an investment for a better present and a brighter future. You might find that practicing meditation requires a lot of struggle and effort. But, meditation is an effortless effort. You need not actively do anything; rather you just need to 'do nothing'. You need not resist anything. You just witness whatever is going on within and remain aware of the knower of everything.

Seeker 2: Life is becoming so hectic that I need to cater to so many demands. How can I practice meditation amidst the problems of life? If we meditate at this point, wouldn't it amount to escaping these situations rather than facing them?

Sirshree: It is common for people to be faced with a profusion of problems that involve relationships, health, financial issues, conflicts in the neighbourhood, difficulties at work, or even issues at the national level. Many people act reactively by jumping to conclusions as soon as problems arise and struggle to solve them. If they are asked to meditate in the midst of such problems, they will consider it to be an escape from reality, exactly as you said.

But nothing could be farther from the truth. *When you meditate, you are free from the clutter of the mind. You are liberated from past beliefs that can influence your approach to your present and future problems.* As you delve deep into meditation, you reach the state of stillness. Your level of consciousness rises. And with a higher awareness, you will observe that the problem has started naturally moving towards the most appropriate solution. This is the power of detached observation, which can only be realized through practice. It is actually a great miracle that each one should witness.

Seeker 3: Some people believe that if they meditate, they will be certain to attain wealth. How true is that?

Sirshree: Meditation is not a means to gain wealth. It is important to understand that meditation will not lead to sudden riches. Unfortunately, some self-proclaimed gurus who are rather spiritual 'entertainers', confound people with such misconceptions. There are priests who preach techniques of increasing wealth in the name of spirituality. Many people are needlessly lured by such techniques and get entangled in these illusions. There is nothing wrong in becoming materially successful. However, meditation has nothing to do with it. The ability to earn or create wealth is different in every body-mind mechanism. Meditation may help in enhancing one's capacity and efficiency at work, but it is not a direct method of getting a good job or becoming rich. But yes, the practice of meditation is surely the way to the experience of pure joy, unshaken peace, love and compassion, which is your true nature.

Seeker 3: I have heard my friends say that meditation should be practiced only in the early hours of the morning. However, my job requires me to travel, making it even more difficult for me to meditate in the morning. What can I do?

Sirshree: Some people avoid meditating because they believe that meditation should be practiced only in the early morning at dawn. As they are not used to waking up so early; they never take to the practice of meditation. Early morning is indeed an auspicious time for meditation. The environment is conducive. There is silence all around. Even your body is supportive as your stomach is empty and your mind is still. If you meditate at that time, you can go deeper into meditation. However, this timing is not mandatory.

You can practice meditation whenever you get up before starting your daily activities. You can surely meditate before retiring for the day, if that suits you.

Seeker 2: Are there other misconceptions that people have about meditation, so that we become aware and are freed from them?

Sirshree: *One very common misconception about meditation is that meditation means sitting with closed eyes like a hermit in the Himalayas, or sitting for hours at one place with eyes closed.* Some people believe that meditation means difficult techniques or self-torture. It is also popularly believed that meditation is for those who are old, and should be practiced after you have retired from active life.

Many people believe that it is necessary to renounce the material world to meditate and to progress on the spiritual path. There are also many who feel it necessary to take a break from productive life to practice meditation. But the converse is true. *Meditation is meant for people from all walks of life and all age groups.* Each and every person can and should meditate, be they student or businessman, householder or pensioner, man or woman, alone as an individual, or in a group. *Meditation can be practiced in solitude or in the marketplace.* And so it is not just for retired or older people. One can practice meditation from childhood. It will only enhance and beautify one's life.

Seeker 2: How can a student benefit from meditation?

Sirshree: When children meditate, their concentration improves and they can perform better in school. Teenagers find that meditation helps them to be more focused and goal-oriented in their studies. Not just students or teenagers, but even people who work in offices find that they have become more relaxed and more efficient at their workplace with meditation. For a homemaker, meditation helps attain harmony in relationships.

The ultimate goal of meditation is to be in the state of love, joy, and peace even when you are in the thick of worldly life at home, at your workplace, at the marketplace; whether you are seated or walking, sleeping or awake, with your eyes closed or open. However, to begin with you can sit in one place, with eyes closed for at least 20 minutes. With consistent practice, you may continue to sit in meditation for a longer duration.

Seeker 3: What is the significance of contemplation and concentration in the context of meditation?

Sirshree: Today the word "meditation" has become so common that the deeper meaning of meditation seems to be lost. "Meditation" is synonymously used with terms such as "reflection" or "contemplation." They are two different terms altogether. In contemplation, you think about a subject from all possible viewpoints. You may first think about the positive aspects of that topic and then focus on its negative aspects. You may want to list down the other aspects and finally, you have an in depth understanding of that subject. But such contemplation is not meditation. Concentration signifies focusing the mind on one particular point to the exclusion of everything else. Meditation is neither a concentration exercise. When the mind is clouded with thoughts, concentration exercises can help in making it sharp, sensitive, and focussed. But, it is important to understand that concentration is not the ultimate goal of meditation. The ultimate goal is to go beyond this.

Seeker 1: People refer to *Pranayama* as a meditation practice. They say that pranayama helps to relax and calm the racing mind.

Sirshree: *Meditation is not relaxation techniques.* Relaxation techniques, such as *Pranayama* or *Shavasana*, help to quieten the body and mind. They can be helpful in preparing the body and mind for meditation. But this altered or relaxed state of mind and body is not meditation.

Understand further that meditation is neither intention, nor self-control, nor willpower exercises. The mind constantly chases after insatiable desires. No sooner does one desire get fulfilled, another arises. You become the slave of the mind by fulfilling these never-ending desires of the mind. By following an intention, or using willpower exercises, you can hold back these desires for a limited time. As a result, your self-control increases. Later, it depends on you whether to fulfil a desire or to give it up. Although these practices will help you to master your mind briefly, this is surely not the goal of meditation. Meditation is essentially the experience of who-you-truly-are.

Seeker 2: Many people say that attuning the body to *Kundalini* (spinal energy) is meditation

Sirshree: Some people believe that awakening the Kundalini is meditation. Kundalini is nothing but energy, located at the base of the spine. Through meditation, this energy rises from the base of the spine through the various chakras in the energy body till the crest of the head. While it does so, it energizes or activates each of the chakras along the way which is called awakening of the Kundalini.

People might perhaps experience deeper empathy with others, or greater sensitivity, higher energy levels and so on.

But true meditation transcends the plane of energy. Meditation is all about experiencing the essence of unmanifest existence that exists beyond all forms of energy. Meditation returns you to pure consciousness, which is the very Source of all creation, beyond all creative energy. If true meditation is your real goal, then it is unnecessary to indulge in practices that concern any such manifest forms of energy.

Seeker 2: I have also heard people taking about out-of-body experiences during meditation. What is the significance of such experiences in meditation?

Sirshree: Astral projection or astral travel is also referred to as an out-of-body experience or OBE. It assumes the existence of an astral body apart from the physical body, which is capable of travelling outside the physical body. All this is in the realm of the mind. *In meditation, both the body and the mind are transcended. Therefore, such experiences are neither meditation nor have anything to do with meditation.*

Seeker 2: I have seen spiritual seekers practicing various rituals during meditation. Are they not meditation?

Sirshree: Yes. There are also such misconceptions that associate meditation with techniques like focusing on the breath or watching your thoughts or performing some rituals. But the techniques that are used for meditation cannot be meditation. There are people who believe that meditation means performing austere acts such as standing on a single foot through day and night. In the process, even if the foot swells, you do not move an inch from your position. Others believe that meditation means penance like lying on a bed of nails, burying the body under the ground up to the neck, not taking food for prolonged periods, or chanting mantras repeatedly. Many others believe that practicing yoga is meditation.

Historically, spiritual seekers in India understood the deeper aspects of meditation. They were established in the supreme bliss of pure consciousness. They practiced yoga and performed penance and austerities, only to experiment whether they could continue to abide in the same blissful state even during a changed state of body. However, as time passed, meditation became wrongly identified with these ritualistic customs and traditions. Some people even practiced these techniques to attain mystical powers. While such practices gained importance, the actual purpose of meditation was lost. *Serious truth seekers, however, focus more on achieving that state of supreme bliss rather than getting involved in such ritualistic practices or their benefits.*

Seeker 2: So then should meditation be practiced only by those who want to attain salvation?

Sirshree: This is yet another misconception that meditation should be practiced only by those who want to attain salvation. But as I mentioned earlier, meditation can and should be practiced by each and every individual. Meditation is like a wish-fulfilling tree. It is up to you how you derive benefit from it. With meditation, you can derive external benefits as well as deeper, spiritual benefit. It can help you gain health and harmony in your relationships and it can also help you to attain true happiness and peace, which is your innate nature. Above all these relative benefits, the real and highest purpose of meditation is to abide in your true self.

Seeker 3: Should meditation be practiced only by people of a particular religion?

Sirshree: You must have heard people saying that they saw an image of God. They believe that meditation means visualizing an image of God. But visualizing involves the activity of the mind. Seeing an image of God is also in the realm of the mind. Further, the image of God is different in different religions. *Meditation is not related to any particular religion. Meditation is your true nature, which is beyond the beliefs and ideologies of all religions. Meditation is universal. True meditation is about experiencing the one who is knowing the witnessing subject, the witnessed world, and also the act of witnessing.* We will learn more about the art of witnessing, so that it becomes a part of our daily routine.

4

Distractions to Self-meditation

Seeker 1: I had never considered these deeper benefits of meditation. I was always so fascinated by the external benefits of meditation that I never thought about these deeper aspects.

Sirshree: This happens with most meditators. Many embark on the journey of meditation, but are so happy with the external benefits that it diverts them from the real purpose.

Seeker 1: Are there any distractions that may take us away from this path? A word of caution can help so that we may not get trapped in them and continue our journey to attain the ultimate goal of meditation.

Sirshree: Yes, there are some distractions that one should be aware of while on this beautiful journey of meditation. One of them is attaining mystical powers.

During meditation, the latent powers of the body are awakened. With these awakened powers the mind becomes extremely focused and concentrated. A focused mind, by itself, is a tremendously powerful force which can generate high energy and can achieve the impossible. However, some people stop their journey and indulge in mystical powers instead of progressing further on the path. *Awakening of latent powers is only an unncessary by-product and not the real goal of meditation. It is also not an essential milestone in the path.* One can attain the ultimate goal of meditation even without these latent powers.

Healing practices are also a kind of distraction in meditation. Meditation is helpful and effective in treating disease. As we have seen earlier, meditation has a great impact on all levels of existence: physical, mental and spiritual. Many diseases like asthma, high or low blood pressure, paralysis, and others have been noted to heal with the practice of meditation. *Meditation has definite positive effects on the body-mind; however, simply achieving better health is not the goal of meditation.* Hence be alert. You may get lured by the superficial benefits of meditation and may make them your final goal. These intermediate benefits may influence you so deeply that they become all you seek.

All these are mere milestones in the journey and not the destination. Being entangled in these allurements is like sitting on the milestones in the path and imagining that you have arrived! *If you stop the practice of meditation at the experience of a relaxed and focused state of mind, or with the awakened powers of the mind, you deprive yourself of attaining the true goal of meditation – the experience and expression of who-you-truly-are.*

Seeker 1: Thank you Sirshree. I will be alert and will stick to the final goal of Self-meditation. I have seen people being involved in practices to awaken the Kundalini energy. I can now see that they are not aware of the real purpose of meditation and continuing to perform rituals with the expectation that something will happen.

Sirshree: That's good. Performing meditation rituals can become a distraction. You might wander away from the path of meditation by assuming them as the destination.

Since ancient times, various rituals or techniques were devised to enter the meditative state. This was because the sense of conscious presence that we truly are is so subtle and close to our essential existence that it cannot be found by the mind that tries to experience it. The experience is so obvious that we easily fail to notice its constant presence.

Let me give you an example. A fish lives in water and there is water all around it. It may search for water wondering where the water is. This may happen because the water is so close to its eyes that it does not even realize that it is in the water. In the same manner, *the experience of conscious being is so close to us that we just do not realize whether it is located within the body or outside. In truth, the experience is space-less and non-localized; it is present everywhere – within and around.*

Furthermore, you don't experience it immediately on closing your eyes for meditation. Hence, to encourage one to persist and abide in the experience of being, Self-realized souls devised various rituals or techniques. But with the passage of time, the real purpose of these rituals or techniques has been lost. People practice these rituals such as breath-watching, or concentrating on the third-eye or agya-chakra or watching changes occurring in the body just as a mere practice. However, as you go deeper in meditation and gain experiential conviction of the Self, such rituals are no longer required. Unfortunately, some people get rooted in such rituals in the name of meditation and don't progress further.

(36) The ego is yet another distraction. *While practicing meditation, people do get engrossed in arousing the latent powers of the body so as to feel superior. As a result, the ego gets a boost bringing arrogance and egotism. There cannot be a bigger fall than this. It leads you to stray from the basic goal of surrendering the ego and knowing who-you-truly-are.* Such enticements, though apparently impressive, result in depriving you of realizing the ultimate truth for which you are actually striving.

Seeker 3: After knowing all this I really feel that what I called meditation was never real mediation.

(37) **Sirshree:** Let's understand what real meditation is. *Real Meditation, which you may call as Self-meditation, is when meditation returns on itself, when awareness is aware of itself. In Self-meditation, you return to the source or awareness. Meditation awakens that source.* Techniques may be helpful in reaching the source of awareness. And when you reach the center, only then can it be said that 'you are in Self-meditation'. Only then is meditation focused on itself.

If you meditate on external objects, it is called attention. But when you turn your meditation within, it is called awareness. *When (38) awareness becomes aware of itself, when the light in which everything is being known shines upon itself that is Self-meditation. Knowing the knower is Self-meditation.*

5

Roadblocks in Meditation

Seeker 1: I feel inspired to practice meditation. But there are times when I really need to push myself to sit in meditation. I find it difficult to sit in meditation; hence I start giving excuses to myself and try to avoid it.

Sirshree: People go through various experiences when they commence the journey of meditation. Sometimes, you might feel too lazy to sit down and meditate. You may consider meditation to be a waste of time and turn to other activities. Even if you sit in meditation, lethargy can overpower to the extent that you may fall asleep while meditating. The mind then gives logical excuses, "As I'm not able to meditate properly, I'll leave it and just go to sleep." Succumbing to this mental logic, you leave the practice midway and go to sleep.

On such a journey, it is inevitable that you will encounter some roadblocks. As we've seen, the mind has no role to play in meditation. Hence, you might struggle with a feeling of boredom initially. You might even equate meditation with boredom. Even a few minutes in meditation might seem like an hour.

Here, you need to understand that *it is the habit of the mind to deceive with logical excuses. As soon as you become aware of this habit and reject it, it will no longer trouble you.* Thereafter, when the mind complains that nothing is happening in meditation, you can tell the mind, "Even if nothing is happening, I will continue to be in meditation as decided." If the mind still tries to get its way, then get up, splash cold water on your face, and resume meditation. *Persisting in the practice without giving up at such moments is the key to success. Resolve to be in meditation for the decided period every day, regardless of obstacles or excuses.*

Eventually, you will see that such obstacles like boredom or lethargy will no longer drift you away. Continuing to practice despite uncomfortable feelings brings its reward. Don't resist the feelings of boredom or lethargy; rather accept them as a part of the practice. If you are unable to accept this and instead keep resisting and fretting over these feelings, then meditation may seem difficult to practice and you might even consider quitting. So, continue to practice meditation and watch such feelings as a detached witness. As you persist with the practice, these feelings will pass away.

Seeker 2: I have been practicing meditation since couple of months now. But I still feel that I am at the very same point where I started the journey. I don't see myself progressing further. Because of this, I have started becoming inconsistent. How should I overcome this?

Sirshree: *Tall expectations and impatience are also roadblocks in meditation that can divert you from your journey.* You may feel impatient to make speedy progress. This impatience is a form of craving or expectation. If you don't notice tangible changes or if progress seems to be slow, you might begin to develop an aversion for the practice. When your predefined expectations are not being met, you may get depressed or vexed, and might begin to make excuses to avoid the practice. You might even doubt your capabilities, or lose confidence in the meditation technique itself. When faced with such roadblocks, you may even think of abandoning the journey!

At such times, remember that every meditator goes through these difficulties. However with perseverance, these impediments gradually disappear. *When you persist in the practice, you begin to realize that all these imagined expectations, incapacities and failures are the antiques of the mind. When you witness the thoughts and feelings by being detached, you can recognize these antiques of the mind and overcome these roadblocks.* This will help you in moving towards the ultimate goal of meditation. You too can experience the immaculate state of love, bliss, and peace that has been sung about and praised by enlightened ones.

Seeker 3: This seemed as if you were actually reading my thoughts. I get bored very soon and hence I give reasons to avoid meditation. I often find myself giving excuses like – I don't think I am able to meditate properly. Leave it. Let's do something else. I will begin meditating when the right time comes.

Sirshree: The right time to mediate is now. What better time than to sit in meditation when you are going through such thoughts! Try and witness those thoughts. Tell your mind, "Come what may, I will continue my journey."

Seeker 3: Right. I get so disappointed that I start doubting whether I am on the right path?

Sirshree: You just touched upon two important points, disappointment and self-doubt. *Disappointment and self-doubt are also barriers that prevent your progress on the journey.*

Some people have a goal-driven attitude towards meditation. There is nothing wrong but, after practicing meditation consistently for a few days, they expect to see some tangible benefits in their life. They have an expectation that this practice will bring in peace of mind, tranquillity, deeper intuition, or greater creativity. When they don't see such results immediately, they get disappointed. They begin to believe that meditation is not helping much, and that it is a futile waste of time. At this point, many seekers quit the practice. The key is, not to hold any such expectations of meditation. *The art of meditation is just to be present and allow any and every feeling or thought to arise and pass.* So, let such feelings of disappointment also pass. Do not hold on to these feelings or resist it.

In the initial stages of the journey, you may experience self-doubt. Questions like: "I am unable to meditate as easily as others do. Am I meditating long enough? Am I meditating correctly? Will I be able to share positive experiences? Am I really eligible to practice meditation?" When you become impatient, want faster results and don't see them coming, you start doubting your capabilities. But such excessive self-analysis will merely create stress and distract you from the real goal. Some people even move from one school of meditation to another in a vain attempt to overcome their doubts. What they don't realize is that as long as doubts continue in the mind, changing meditation schools will serve no purpose. So just witness these thoughts of doubt as they arise. They will soon fade away.

Seeker 2: I too go through many such thoughts that make me very restless during meditation. As you mentioned earlier, thoughts overpower to the extent that I leave the practice midway.

Sirshree: Sometimes you may find that your mind is racing during meditation. Thoughts about the recent past or near future may constantly flood your awareness. Such thoughts may even consume the entire meditation session. Being frustrated, you might even blame the practice of meditation, considering it to be unhelpful. But you need to understand that this surge of thoughts is just a reflection of the restless mind and not a consequence of meditation. The fact that the surge of thoughts appears intense only indicates that your awareness is rising and that you are able to notice them. Treat it as a sign of progress, rather than failure.

When you engage in intense activities just before meditation, your energy levels are high. Meditation is about stillness. When sitting in the stillness of meditation, your mind will still be attached to those energetic thoughts. Hence, you may find that your mind is full of thoughts. *It is only through meditation that you become aware of this restlessness of the mind, which otherwise would have gone unnoticed.* Hence it is important to continue to practice meditation despite these thoughts. Rather witness the thoughts as they are.

Seeker 1: This might sound a little weird, but when I sit for meditation, I get distracted by the faintest of sounds and open my eyes to see what's going on. Even the odour of food being cooked does not let me focus on the meditation. How do I focus then?

Sirshree: This is because of the senses that gravitate towards sense-objects. Although they are here to help us stabilize in our true nature, senses also become one of the most important roadblocks that you should be aware off. As soon as you court the pleasures of the senses you lose yourself in them. Your ears get absorbed by melodious music, eyes are captivated by enchanting sights, and tongue craves delicious tastes. You are intoxicated by sweet fragrances and also get lost in the feeling of delicate touch. The mind revels in intellectual delights. In short, you seek and constantly entangle yourself in all kinds of sensual pleasures. However, the underlying point is that all these are nothing but roadblocks in the journey of meditation. And as we discussed earlier, meditation will only help you have better control over senses.

There is one more important truth that we need to understand. The true purpose of the senses is to bring awareness of who-we-truly-are. Viewing the world informs us that we have eyes. Hearing sounds informs us that we have ears. Taste and smell remind us of the presence of tongue and nose. *Experiencing sights, sounds, tastes, smells, and touch should also remind us of the true purpose of these senses. Your attention is absorbed by the objects of the senses; instead, they should lead you to the awareness of the presence of the senses themselves.* You are deluded into believing that these sense objects are merely for pleasure. But for those seeking enlightenment, they are only a means to direct the attention to the knower of everything. In spiritual terms, it can be called Self-witnessing. Such external sense objects are the means to witness the Self and thus abide in the sense of being.

As the senses stimulate thoughts in the mind, you should be aware of the knower who is witnessing those thoughts. The knower is always awake, aware, and conscious of those thoughts. Our sensory perceptions are signals to connect to this supreme source of knowing. It is due to ignorance that we accept the illusion of our perceptions but miss the news of conscious presence that they are constantly conveying to us. As a result, we are entrapped by whatever our senses perceive instead of knowing the knower of everything.

But the good news is: These hindrances are nothing but the teething troubles that occur only in the initial stages of meditation. If you meditate consistently despite such hindrances, this phase will soon pass away. You will attain the subtler depth of meditation and can easily meditate for a longer period. As you derive the bliss that is inherent in meditation, you will be convinced to practice this daily, just as you are convinced that you should take a bath every day. With the passage of time, whenever you get the chance, take the opportunity to dip into this inner stillness. Nobody will even notice as you briefly connect within, but this practice will make life easy and effortless.

Seeker 2: This really clears most of my doubts. I often find myself in the state of peace and bliss. But it happens that there is a small emotion related to some past incident that suddenly arises. The peace that I was experiencing seems to vanish. At times, it is just some thought about my future. That thought slowly pulls me in and I get so involved in those thoughts that I even forget that I was ever meditating. But now with this clarity, I will be able to meditate better.

Sirshree: Great! Let me tell you a small story that will summarize all this and will also clear any doubts that you all might still have.

You all have seen carnivals. So imagine a carnival procession is trouping through the main street of the town. To get a better view of the procession, you visit your friend, whose apartment is located on the same street. The balcony of the apartment looks onto the street where the carnival is proceeding. Many people have gathered there to watch the colourful procession.

Now, as you are watching and enjoying the beautiful procession from the balcony, some children behind you begin to pull your shirt and poke you with many questions. You get distracted and cannot enjoy the procession. Unwillingly, you answer them. But, they don't stop there. They have more and more questions that disturb you. In agitation, you leave the balcony and go to the neighbour's apartment to view the procession.

In this apartment, there are some elderly people who are constantly coughing. As they see you there, they too start asking you questions. Now you begin addressing their questions. But as they are old, they cannot hear your answers clearly. There are some youngsters in the other room playing loud music and hence you have to shout to make yourself heard. Soon, you feel distracted by all this and decide to move on to the next apartment.

In the next apartment, you are listening to the angry quarrels of the family who stay there. You cannot enjoy the procession from their balcony either. So, as a last resort, you visit the last apartment with a balcony over the street. Now, the ladies there are troubled by their noisy children and are busy scolding the children.

So, now what can you do? Every house you visit disturbs you in one way or the other. It seems you're not going to be able to witness the procession and enjoy it after all.

In this story, the building represents the body-mind. When you sit in meditation, you use the body-mind as a medium to experience the Self. This experience is signified by the witnessing of the carnival procession. However, after a while you get distracted by the thoughts of the restless mind. This is represented by the children who keep distracting your attention. They conjure thoughts of fear and ambition, which pull you out of the meditative state. The elderly people symbolize the discomfort you experience in the body. Pain in the legs, shoulders, or spine distracts you from the peace and bliss of meditation. The quarrelling neighbours represent feelings of hatred and ill-will. Indulging in thoughts over arguments and making comparisons with others keeps you away from the experience of the Self. The ladies scolding their children signify thoughts of attachment. Thoughts of attachment towards objects or people cloud the clarity of the mind. Finally, the street represents life in this world. When one lacks proper understanding, worldly obstacles distract them from the experience of the Self. However, with right understanding, the same obstacles become instrumental and serve as a medium to know the original state of being, to realize who-you-truly-are.

Seeker: That's such a perfect analogy! This is exactly what happens with me. I think of an incident and then the entire chain of thoughts with associated feelings of anger, guilt etc. follow. In frustration or to avoid them, I stop meditating.

Sirshree: True. As you lead your life, you go through a variety of experiences. These trigger a whole range of emotions such as anger, anxiety, attachment, boredom, confusion, depression, doubt, ego, fear, greed, guilt, hatred, ill-will, impatience, insecurity, jealousy, and lust in the body. You either express them or suppress them.

But when you continue to sit in meditation, the conscious mind, which has been active all the time, slows down. You start becoming aware of the subtler aspects of the body-mind mechanism, such as the breath, emotions, thoughts and various other body sensations. You begin to witness the chain of thoughts and emotions passing through. In the process, certain thoughts trigger the suppressed emotions within you. They manifest as pleasurable, painful or neutral sensations on the body.

During meditation, you should witness these thoughts, emotions, and sensations with equanimity. You neither suppress nor express them. When you begin to observe the emotions with equanimity, you will then be liberated from them forever. When you react to these emotions by favouring them or resisting them, they are reinforced. Indulging in these emotions then gives rise to further thoughts. Thus, the cycle continues.

When a thought of anxiety arises, you add further thoughts to the worry. You might start recollecting all the pending activities and start feeling the concern towards them. When you become aware that you've been distracted, you then focus on meditation again. Thoughts of fear, greed, jealousy, or insecurity can distract you. You can also be distracted by recurring self-checking to analyze your state, or in taking credit for achieving a thoughtless state. Then some new ideas arise which you feel are important, but fear that you will forget those ideas.

These recurring thoughts then give rise to doubts like, "Am I meditating correctly?" You may begin comparing the ongoing meditation session with a previous session. If you find too many thoughts are racing through the mind, you might feel dissatisfied at not experiencing an earlier peaceful state. Thoughts of depression then add themselves to the mental worries. You may begin to feel unworthy or incapable of reaching a higher spiritual state. Random thoughts of these kinds continue to arise in the restless mind. As this happens, you tend to forget that you were seated to witness all these emotions, thoughts and sensations and use them as a medium to be conscious of the awareness in which all these arise.

Hence, as part of the preparation for meditation, consider the way to handle all these obstacles. Then during meditation, witness them with equanimity, alertness and understanding. *Regardless of the variety of emotions, sensations of pleasure or pain on the body, or thoughts of craving or aversion, you should have the underlying understanding that these are temporary. They have emerged, will remain for a while and will subside. Therefore, instead of indulging in them, treat them as a game and use them as an instrument to know the knower of everything.* This way, you can break free from them and abide in the experience of the true witnessor.

6

Preparing for Meditation

Seeker 1: You mentioned about prior preparation of the mind for meditation. What is significance of such preparation?

Sirshree: *Preparation helps you in going deeper in meditation. Preparation leads to readying the mind to be still.* The mind is a bundle of thoughts. They are very similar to the waves in the ocean. The waves originate from the ocean, exist for some time, and then perish back into the ocean. Similarly, thoughts arise from the ocean of consciousness. They come alive for some time and then dissolve into the ocean. No thought is permanent. Numerous thoughts run through the mind from dawn to night. Most of our energy gets exhausted by giving attention to these thoughts. When you sit in meditation with such a mind, it won't allow you to go deeper within. Hence, it is necessary to prepare the mind before beginning meditation so as to attain deeper attunement.

Seeker 2: How do we prepare our mind?

Sirshree: Let's understand how to prepare the mind to go deeper in meditation.

The most conducive time for meditation is early morning when you've had good sleep and the mind is still and calm. But as we've understood earlier, it can be practiced even during the day.

The first step is to relax your mind. It's better to slow down your activities before meditation so that the mind becomes relaxed. Before you sit for meditation, talk to the mind, "I was in a hurry earlier, but now I am going to slow down my activities." For the best results, plan your daily schedule in such a way that you avoid any last minute rush. It is good if you can fix a daily timeslot for meditation, so that the mind is attuned for this timeslot.

The mind can be relaxed by observing the breath. You don't need to regulate your breath. Neither do you need to breathe rapidly nor take long, deep breaths. Breathe naturally. *When the breathing is natural and when you observe your breath, the mind automatically calms down.* This is beneficial not only to relax your mind but also has a very good effect on your overall health.

Seeker 2: Is there any other technique of relaxation?

Sirshree: Besides breath-watching, you can also practice visualization. Sit in a comfortable posture. Take a deep breath and release it slowly. To relax your mind further, visualise a beautiful pleasant scene that you like. It could be of a beautiful garden, a beach, or a natural waterfall cascading down a mountain where you had been for a picnic. Let your eyes wander in that scene. Pay attention to all the important details in that scene. When your mind has seen and experienced the complete scene, check the state of your body. Is there tension in any part of the body? You will notice that your body has become relaxed. If there is still tension in any part of the body, contract that part and then let it loose again. Then instruct that part: "Release the tension… relax… relax… relax…" In this way, release the tension from the arms, legs, shoulders, back, knees and eyes. This technique is an effective method for relaxation of the body. Once the body is relaxed the next step is prayer.

Seeker 3: Prayer!? How does prayer help in meditation?

Sirshree: Prayer has tremendous power. It can stop a storm. It can bring a sinking ship ashore.

Prayer invokes the desire to be liberated from all other desires. When you are free from all desires, you attain a thoughtless state in which the true understanding of who-you-truly-are awakens. When you pray before meditation, you surrender all your problems and worries in the hands of God, the creator. You become receptive to the grace that is being bestowed on you during meditation. *Prayer is a medium through which you speak to God, and God answers the prayer through meditation.* Prayer helps to create the feelings that will ease the process of entering the state of meditation. When you are completely absorbed in meditation, real prayer begins. You begin to achieve the aim that you wanted to attain through meditation. At this stage, prayer and meditation, both become one. You may say that prayer is the beginning and it ends in meditation.

Seeker 3: Is there any specific prayer or ritual that should be performed?

Sirshree: You can pray in whatever way you are accustomed. You may use your own words but the feelings associated with the prayer are of prime importance. You can invoke these feelings through gestures like joining the palms near the heart, or raising your hands up, or any other body gesture that you are familiar with. Remember to immerse yourself in prayer with complete feeling. The more feeling you put into your prayer, the better will be the result.

There is one more invocation or prayer that you may want to perform before performing your chosen prayer. This will help in making yourself receptive. It is called the Bright prayer. It is an invocation that you do for meditation to bear the most positive fruit. The Bright prayer is as follows:

The prayer I will now recite will have the most positive effect on my body and mind.

Now, repeat the prayer you have chosen in which you have faith. Alternatively, you may repeat the prayer given below with complete peace, love, deep feeling, faith and rhythm. This prayer has tremendous power to relax your mind.

I am peaceful in the presence of Divine Silence.
I am experiencing complete peace.
I am created by God.
Therefore peace and bliss,
which are the nature of God,
are spreading within my heart and mind.
God has created nothing to disrupt this peace.
Whatever may be the reason of my unrest
is not in the list of the Almighty.
I am surrendering myself in his lap
just like a tired child rests in its mother's lap.
Waves of joy are arising within and all around me.

I am feeling a sense of deep peace everywhere.
Peace... Peace... Peace...

Once this is done, the mind will calm down and begin to focus.

Seeker 1: How do we increase this focus so that we go deeper in meditation?

Sirshree: Through contemplation. Although contemplation is not meditation, it helps in knowing the depth of a particular topic. It is yet another technique to focus the mind. Certain difficult things can be easily understood through contemplation.

Without contemplation, you may not realize the value of the priceless spiritual knowledge that you've gained. It would remain as mere information. *Without contemplation, even diamonds are mere pieces of coal.* Every stone when polished with the tool of contemplation has the possibility of becoming a gemstone.

When you contemplate the deeper truths of life and your true nature, your mind becomes conducive to access inner stillness. The purer the contemplation, the faster you reach the state of inner stillness. However, if you contemplate on other topics that lead you to the external world, then the mind tends to become cluttered, making it difficult to access inner stillness.

Seeker 2: Are there any such topics that can be contemplated, so as to lead us to stillness? Can you give some examples?

Sirshree: The questions that will help you contemplate could be:

What is the eye of the eye? What is the ear of the ear? Who is knowing these thoughts?

How was your face before you were born? How was your face before your parents were born?

You could also contemplate on topics like death. Death is a long sleep; and sleep is a short death. Don't die before dying. Instead of dying every day out of fear, it is better to die only once in life.

The strength to solve problems has been given to us before the problems arise. Even before a child is born, nature arranges for its nutrition.

God or Consciousness is present within everyone.

Sorrow does not appear in your life to make you unhappy. Sorrow comes to awaken you.

Arousal of desire is not the cause of sorrow. When the mind becomes identified with desire, then the identification becomes the cause of sorrow.

If you keep thinking or ponder on such topics for long, initially you could get wrong answers, but later you may get the right answers.

All these will help you in your contemplation. Consistency is the key to success. Remember that meditation should be practiced regularly and consistently. Meditate at least once or twice a day. Even a day's break can make you lethargic and may become the cause of laziness. With consistency, the mind becomes accustomed to meditation. As a result, you will notice that as soon as you sit in meditation, the mind has become calm and reaches the depth of meditation. Then meditation will become an integral part of your life, just like breathing.

You also need to tell the mind to be patient during meditation. Let it not be concerned whether or not the thoughtless state is being

attained. The mind's tendency is such that it begins to imagine the thoughtless state and keeps checking whether or not that state has been attained. It may believe that the meditation session is successful only when a thoughtless state is achieved. There could be times when there may be painful sensations on the body or drowsiness that makes you fall asleep during meditation. The mind may assume that the session is a failure. So it's important to instruct the mind that no such thing is true. *A successful meditation session is one in which thoughts, body sensations, and emotions are observed from the perspective of a detached witness. Self-experience is possible, regardless of the presence or absence of body sensations, emotions and thoughts.* Therefore, there is no need to worry about the results of meditation. As you said earlier, thoughts related to new ideas or solutions to problems may arise during meditation and the mind may start pondering them. Instruct the mind in the beginning of the session that you will be giving separate time for them later, although they may be of interest. The present time is meant only for meditation. *By practicing meditation, you are giving an opportunity to the Self to know itself.*

The mind may try to mechanically perform meditation as a ritual or may get stuck in the technique itself. Therefore, tell the mind not to be stuck with the process. With proper understanding, the mind then prepares to surrender its preconditions and allow meditation to naturally unfold.

7

The Art of Witnessing

Seeker 1: As you said, while we witness our thoughts, we should neither express the triggered programmed reactions nor should we suppress them. We should just witness them as they are. I would like to understand what needs to be done in such witnessing.

Sirshree: During meditation, dormant past impressions ingrained within from behaviour learned since childhood, get activated and appear in conscious awareness as thoughts, emotions or body sensations. You tend to either suppress or express them as per your past conditioning.

When you witness the thoughts, emotions and sensations with the right understanding it is said to be true witnessing. With true witnessing, they are permanently released from the body-mind. As a result, your body–mind gets truly purified. Here, witnessing doesn't mean seeing with open eyes. Witnessing is just knowing your reactions and being detachedly aware of them as they arise and subside.

Seeker 1: What is true witnessing?

Sirshree: *True witnessing involves the three essential aspects – Understanding, Awareness and Equanimity.*

 Understanding: The most important understanding is that who-you-truly-are is separate from the body-mind. You are the Self – pure consciousness – who is using the body-mind as a medium to experience itself and express its divine qualities. During meditation, your body-mind is cleansed and begins to serve as a mirror for the Self to know itself. Here, understanding implies a firm experiential conviction that all thoughts, emotions and body sensations are happening with the body-mind... not with who-you-truly-are.

The other key aspect of understanding is to know that everything that arises at the level of the body-mind is temporary. Every thought or feeling is like a flare shot in the night sky. A flare is a trail of light that rises up in the night sky, exists for a few moments and then dissolves into the dark. In the same way, thoughts and feelings arise from the space-less presence that you truly are. They show up for a few moments and then dissolve into the silent stillness of the presence. You need to develop a firm conviction that all thoughts and feelings are temporary in nature. With this conviction, you will stop reacting to them by giving them undue importance. This does not mean that you become heedless to the needs of the body. The body will receive due care and attention to heal it and keep it functioning in the best possible way. However, you will no longer overreact or indiscriminately get entangled in thoughts or emotions.

 The second aspect of true witnessing is that of Awareness. As we spoke earlier, when you are not aware during meditation, you lose yourself in thoughts, emotions and body sensations that arise during meditation. The mind spends most of its time in fantasies and illusions. It chews over the experiences of the past. It attempts to re-live either the joy of pleasurable experiences or the worries and regrets of unpleasant ones. As a result, you get distracted from meditation. If you develop the ability to be aware of the present moment, you can immediately detach yourself from them and be aware of the Self.

(63) *The last aspect is that of Equanimity. Treat everything with an attitude of evenness; an alike manner which is beyond like and dislike, aversion and craving.* Look at pain and pleasure, success and failure, fame and shame, praise and blame, all with evenness. They all are temporary and have come to go. Just watch them with (64) equanimity while they are there. *Equanimity builds the ability to witness all thoughts, emotions, and body sensations for what they truly are.*

Seeker 2: In the above context, how do we then witness thoughts?

Sirshree: During meditation, you may find that thoughts of the recent past or the near future are perhaps incessantly arising. New ideas may also arise. Pursuing these thoughts distracts you from meditation. It's only when you regain awareness that you realize that you had been distracted. In such a situation, if you don't attain a thoughtless state, you might assume your meditation session to be a failure.

The body, as we all know, is a thinking machine. Thoughts keep arising in it. You never know which thoughts may arise and when. A new thought can pop up at any moment, and you could get entangled in it. If you carefully observe, you can feel these thoughts just the same way as you feel your clothes on your body, just as you feel the air from a blowing fan. These thoughts are very much a part of the body. However, who-you-truly-are is distinct from the body.

So what you need to do is to watch the thoughts arising in the body from a detached point of view. Let me give you an example: If a note with the word "Anger" was stuck on your forehead, how would you perceive it? Would you feel the emotion? No. You would only feel the presence of that note on the forehead. Whatever word has been written on the note will have no affect on you.

Similarly, perceive your thoughts in the same way as you would feel the note. Watch all the thoughts and emotions arising within the body as a note on the body. Thoughts can be viewed just like any other thing, unless you give exaggerated meaning to the content that they carry. Ignore the content of the thoughts and just see the thoughts for what they truly are. These thoughts and emotions arise to tell you that who-you-truly-are is separate from the body. They are here only to remind you of your essential presence.

Witness thoughts in the same way as you watch files opening on a laptop. When you open a file in your laptop, it does not mean it is opened within you. That file is simply opened in the machine you are using.

In the same way, *thoughts and emotions are like various files that are being opened in the body you are using. They occur in the body, but you exist beyond the body.* Your true nature is pure consciousness – the source of everything. Once you develop this conviction through your own experience, you will be able to quickly detach yourself from emotions and thoughts.

Seeker 3: I am beginning to understand what witnessing means. How can we practice witnessing, especially when we are going through a turmoil of disturbing emotions?

Sirshree: Whenever emotions arise, the first step is to observe your body sensations and breath. When any emotion arises in the body, the first thing that changes is the breathing and the heart pulse rate. Both change when we are emotionally aroused. Let's take an example of anger. When a person is angry or an emotion of anger has arisen, what are the physical changes that take place on the body. Your breath becomes rapid and shallow, ears become warm and the heart beats rapidly. You feel a pressure in the forehead or in the chest. There is a sudden tension in the arms, neck, or shoulders. These sensations are nothing but the body's reactions to the thought that triggered anger. Typically, you tend to identify yourself with these sensations, and because of the discomfort and resistance, you try to escape it by either bursting out into expressions of anger or suppressing it forcefully.

So now, as a part of your training, as soon as you sense an emotion arising within you, tell yourself, "Let me see if this emotion is really being experienced by me or if it has arisen in this body." Just like the example of the scissor, are these emotions happening to the body, the tool that you are using? Or are they happening to who-you-truly-are? As soon as you ask this question, you will get the answer that the emotion is within the body, not with me – not with who-I-truly-am. When you are able to see this clearly, then you are in the highest state of meditation.

The body sensations and breathing may vary with each emotion. So witness these changes relentlessly in a detached manner; watch them die down just as waves disappear in the ocean. These sensations and breathing are part of the body; who-you-truly-are is separate from them. They are helping you to know the source of all this.

Seeker 3: This is indeed helpful. How should we witness our body sensations in meditation?

Sirshree: When you sit in meditation you experience various sensations on the body such as heat, cold, heaviness, lightness, dryness, pressure, pain, itching, throbbing, sweating, tickling, twitching, contraction, expansion, vibration, or anything else. You may also experience lightness or heaviness in certain parts of the body or painful sensations in your legs, neck, shoulders, arms or eyes. Some sensations are due to physical aches and pains, while others arise as an aftermath of emotions. You try to escape these sensations by changing your body posture, by scratching an itch, or stretching some muscles. You do this based on past conditioning of the mind. But when you do so, you get distracted from meditation. *What you resist persists. So, if you resist these sensations, they will persist. Therefore, reacting excessively to dismiss these temporary sensations is futile. You need to keep in mind that it is normal for the body to experience various sensations.* There is nothing special about them. It really doesn't matter much if the heaviness in the body persists till the end of the meditation session. Know that who-you-truly-are is separate from such sensations of heaviness or lightness.

The sensations you experience are temporary. They have arisen, will remain for some time, and then perish. Just witness them with equanimity. When you are able to witness these sensations with equanimity it indicates that you are progressing in meditation. If you like one sensation and dislike the other, it means that you are caught by by your past programming and need to continue the practice of meditation consistently..

In reality, the painful sensations that you experience in meditation are not as intense as you believe them to be. Brush aside the beliefs that disguise how you perceive the pain and experience it as it actually is. There is no need to experience the suffering that comes with painful sensations. *Persevere through the pain while the sensation lasts. Pain indicates the release of certain habits and tendencies borne out of past conditioning. It's a common adage that there are no gains without pains. But the truth is that you truly gain only by "understanding" pain for what it actually is.*

Successful meditation involves witnessing all body sensations with equanimity and knowing the knower of all these experiences. The knower is separate from the sensations of the body.

The body is an instrument to reflect the presence of the Self. Defocus from the body to avoid getting entangled in body sensations. *Use such sensations as a bridge to shift awareness to the experience of the Self.* The body is like a mirror for the Self. Regardless of mood, memories, weather, or surroundings, the body can become a medium for the Self to experience itself.

Seeker 1: I can see that my mind plays tricks. It begins to question the state of mind. In a vain attempt to quieten the mind, I try finding answers and this leads to a never-ending volley of questions.

Sirshree: (Laughing) Let's understand how to deal with these and other such thoughts.

During meditation, questioning thoughts may occur, such as: why do I have so many thoughts? When will a thoughtless state emerge? Why do I feel heaviness in the beginning and lightness later on? Some of these thoughts are simply checking whether you are meditating or have gone asleep. The mind continuously questions, because the mind is not yet matured in the practice of meditation. It is still like a child.

Imagine you are travelling with a child in a train. The child peers through the window and starts asking many questions. "What is this?... What is that?... Why is it like this, or that?" You gently answer the questions and enjoy doing so. You don't become engrossed in what the child is pointing out. Similarly, if questioning thoughts arise, understand that this is normal. Consider it as the mind's mischief, and smile. Treat such questions as any other thoughts. Without getting stuck in such thoughts, focus your attention on the sense of being. You can also defocus from your thoughts by focusing on your breath. As you focus on breathing in and breathing out, you become aware of the present moment.

Seeker 2: What are the other thoughts that might distract during a meditation session?

Sirshree: The mind plays many tricks. While meditating, thoughts of anger or hatred may arise. But when you start witnessing, you will be able to overcome them. You will experience the state of silence and peace. Now at this juncture, there could be yet another thought that tries to inform you about this state. Consider that thought too as a part of the scene. Eg. While you are in this state, suddenly a thought may arise, "What a beautiful state this is! I have never experienced such a peaceful state before." Understand that this thought too is trying to distract you from the state of pure awareness. Again, treat it as one of those many thoughts. With this, you will be able to remain in the state of pure awareness.

When you go deep into meditation, the next trick that the mind plays is that it starts checking or tries to judge the experience. You can call this the checker mind. The checker mind assesses, "Let me see who is experiencing this experience. Is this experience the same as the actual experience of the Self?... Nothing is happening. After sitting for so long, why am I not becoming thoughtless?" The mind tries to divert your focus from the experience of the Self by checking, comparing, and judging. If you get entangled in this, you lose your attention on the Self and instead become entrapped in the checker mind's exploits.

So then, what do you do? Whenever the checker mind intervenes, know that it is a trap.

Let's say: Someone is inside a washroom. You want to know whether the washroom is vacant. So, you enquire, "Is there anyone inside?" The person replies, "No." Do you then believe that no one is inside? Or do you conclude that there is someone inside? The reply, by itself, indicates that there is someone in the washroom.

During meditation, the checker mind questions the existence of Self. However, the checker mind can't exist without the Self as it originates from the Self. Thus, its very presence indicates the presence of the Self. Hence, *whenever a checker thought arises, simply smile and observe it. Know that the mind is playing a trick. Understand that you don't have to question the experience; you only need to be present in that experience.*

The checker mind needs to be countered with the understanding that it is enough to witness the play of thoughts, emotions and body sensations in a detached manner instead of determining specific results.

With this understanding you will realize that the checker mind is not qualified to check the experience. The experience of the Self is beyond the domain of the checker mind. The mind can never fathom it. If you believe what the checker mind is saying, you will get entangled in it and will lose your attention on the Self. Whenever the checker mind appears, instead of fighting or debating with it, just smile and acknowledge its presence.

Here's an example that will help you understand this. You are wearing a pair of spectacles and can see everything clearly. Then suddenly the spectacles start questioning, "Let me see who is watching through me. What is my watcher's shape and form?" You know very well that the spectacles can never see the one that is seeing through them.

When the checker mind gets triggered, ask the checker some questions like: Do you know what the experience of Self is like? If not, would you be capable of understanding it if it was explained to you? Is your claim to knowledge within your realm of experience? Or is it only when you are not there that the experience reveals itself? If you ask these questions repeatedly, you will notice that the checker disappears, allowing the experience of Self to be revealed. There will be a time when the checker becomes mature. It will then say, "Now, I will keep quiet. I understand that the experience is beyond my realm of knowing."

The power of faith and devotion will help you in and through the process of abiding in the experience of the Self. Though you have not attained that experience, you should trust and abide with this faith. Have faith in the knowledge about the nature of the checker. Some people find it easy to transcend the checker. Others may need to convince the checker repeatedly. There will be a time when the checker surrenders out of devotion. It then says, "Thy will is my will." The body-mind then merely serves as a mirror for the Self to know itself and express its qualities.

Until you experience this for yourself, you need to know that the checker is indeed the biggest obstacle to the experience of the Self. As you continue with meditation, without asking any questions, you can achieve this conviction in practice. Then you will no longer become drawn by the commentary of the mind. With this, you move to the next level of meditation. But until then, you need to continue with your practice.

Sirshree: There is one more very important trick that the mind plays that you all should be aware off?

Seeker 3: What would that be?

Sirshree: *As soon as you attain the first experience of beingness in meditation, the mind inevitably arrives in the form of a credit-taker. A credit-taker is the one who takes credit of all doing. It tries to play with the experience and take ownership.* The mind tries to own the experience of the Self and will attempt to use it for its own benefit by saying, "I did it… I attained the experience of the Self".

Whenever the credit-taker thought arises, understand this is just one more trick of the mind. Make the mind understand, "You can't make use of the experience. It is only when you were absent that the experience was revealed. Therefore, you need to surrender yourself for the experience to be revealed again. To the extent that you remain still, the experience will shine forth. The more you chatter, the greater the delay in attaining the experience of the Self."

When both the credit-taker and the checker surrender, the individual ego ceases to exist. The body-mind then becomes instrumental for the experience and expression of the Self.

Seeker 3: Once during meditation I experienced a blissful state of thoughtless silence. But that was just once and shortlived. I tried a lot but never got the same experience again.

Sirshree: As you progress in meditation, new dimensions unfold each day. Sometimes you may feel you have had a particularly pleasant or unusual experience. You then mistakenly want to hold on to that experience, and expect to experience the same in your next meditation session. In doing so, you jump to conclusions and try to pre-determine the result of your meditation session. You try to fix the end result.

You should understand that whatever happens during meditation is quite normal. You should not become fixated about any one thing. *Every meditation session is unique in itself. Let whatever is happening happen, and let whatever is not happening not happen. When you are able to know the knower of the result, then that is true progress.* If you see a particular light during meditation, then know the seer who is watching the light. If you hear a special sound, then know the knower of that sound. *The ultimate goal of meditation is not to know any experiences you may have, but to know the knower of those experiences.*

And finally, understand that the journey you have undertaken should be pleasant. Happiness is not just derived from reaching the destination. Hence, it is important to know who is meditating – who you actually are. *Who-you-truly-are is the original cause of true happiness. So, you can be happy even while you journey on this path.*

8

Sense of Being

Seeker 1: The art of witnessing really helped in going deep in meditation. You explained how the body is different from who-I-truly-am. What is our true nature? How is the experience or consciousness? If I am that consciousness, why is it that we don't feel it?

Sirshree: In meditation, you become aware of who-you-truly-are through true witnessing. *Who-you-truly-are is the living presence. Presence is the basis of existence. It is the wakeful awareness of life itself. It is your true nature. The sense of presence is the simple truth that you are constantly and spontaneously aware of.*

It is because we are present that we engage in all activities. E.g. I am eating, I am writing, I am reading etc. I am comes first. It is because "I am" that I am eating, writing, reading etc. and I am aware that I am writing". We tend to be lost in whatever follows "I am…" Everything that follows I am is subject to change. I am a man, I am a woman, I am sad, I am happy, I am a writer etc. But what still remains constant is "I am" It is this "I am", this constant sense of presence that enlivens all activities of life. As we had discussed earlier, presence is the most obvious experience. It is the open secret – so open and obvious that we easily fail to notice it.

Seeker 1: How can we fail to notice something that is so obvious!?

Sirshree: Suppose a soft sound is constantly playing in the background during the day while you are engrossed in your daily activities. You soon get habituated to it. After a few hours, you lose awareness of this sound, even though it continues to play. It is only when the sound stops momentarily that you become aware of its existence.

Similarly, the sense of our presence is ceaselessly going on ever since we are born. We change our identity – from being a child to becoming an adolescent, from being a youth to a middle – aged family maker, from a student to one who earns a living, from being a parent to being a grandparent. However this sense of being remains unchanged, it is constant.

Being aware of this presence and abiding in it lends completeness to meditation. *Meditation becomes 100% when the witnessor returns on itself, when the witnessor witnesses the witnessor-self. 100% Meditation is when you shift from witnessing the world to Self-witnessing; it is the state of being absorbed in Self; when awareness is absorbed in itself.*

Seeker 1: Wow! This is indeed a missing link in the practice of meditation. Prevalent practices like mindfulness aim at detaching ourselves by witnessing our activities and the world. But I am now able to understand that we have to shift our attention on the one who is witnessing.

Seeker 2: If presence is experienced in the stillness beyond thoughts, then what is the role of thoughts in life?

Sirshree: *Ultimately, thoughts – whether they are trivial and mundane, or brilliant and revolutionary – serve merely as a medium to indicate that presence of the source.* This is the whole and sole purpose of thoughts. Thoughts indicate that you are present. With consistent practice of meditation, you will be able to rest in the pure presence.

Shift your attention from the body-mind to consciousness within. Turn back your attention from objects of perception to that which enables perception, from thought to that which enables thinking. You will then rise above the changing and limited to that which is changeless, eternal and boundless.

There is nothing to be *done* to experience presence. When you abide in awareness of presence, you go beyond the body. Bodily sensations may continue to be felt, actions may happen, but there will be a constant awareness of this formless presence of just being alive.

Seeker 2: How can we sense inner stillness when we are experiencing aches and discomfort in the body?

Sirshree: We can sense our beingness through the medium of the body. The sense of the body and the sense of being i.e. the sense of wakeful presence co-exist. There may be painful sensations on the body. Despite these, we need to place our attention on the existence of who-we-truly-are.

It is a myth that meditation can be successful only when you lose of body sensations. If the sense of the body is lost during meditation that is just a bonus, but it is not the real aim. People get entangled in this aim due to this misunderstanding. Had it been true, people suffering from pains would have never attained Self-realization. In fact, we can focus on the sense of our being despite painful sensations on the body.

What happens when we sleep? Every night we lose the sense of the body when we sleep, yet we are not delighted about it when we get up in the morning. *Merely losing the sense of the body is of no use if there is no recognition of the sense of being.* People have many such experiences, but inwardly they remain the same. Therefore, *during meditation, we should train our attention on the sense of being, and not on the sense of body or the lack of it.* Before meditation, we should instruct ourselves not to be disturbed by the sense of body remaining during meditation. We can then be in meditation with ease.

The body is helping us to sense our beingness every moment. We are pure being; the body is only a pretext to know this beingness. In ignorance, we identify ourselves with the limited form of the body. However, our true nature is boundless, vast, much beyond the limited confines of the body. As the body is helping you know your nature, give it a pat on the back and say, "You're doing a good job. Be present next to me so that I can experience my true nature and express my qualities through you."

Nevertheless, if there are habits, tendencies and disorders in the body, the body will not support you during meditation. It will react according to its old programming, and you will find yourselves drawn into the details of the body–mind. You will get entangled in thoughts, emotions and body sensations and the sense of being diminishes. You need to work on the patterns of the body that draw your attention, you need to break its tendencies and habits, in order to stabilize in the experience of the Self.

85. *Meditation will help in being stabilized in this sense of being, in the state of who-you-truly-are. When you transcend all the thoughts, feelings and sensations, you will be able to experience that presence. Then it can be said that meditation is meditating on itself.*

9

The Thoughtless State

Seeker 1: While practicing meditation, I rarely find a few moments when there are no thoughts. Is it possible to have a absolutely thoughtless state of being?

Sirshree: This question arises because you consider the thoughtless state to be the gap between thoughts. However, as we have already discussed earlier, *the silence of beingness exists not just between thoughts, but also "behind" thoughts. This presence is the constant background screen on which thoughts rise and fall.* If you want to call this the "thoughtless state", then it can be considered that you are already thoughtless. There is no need to explicitly bring the thoughtless state. When you practice meditation consistently, you will develop the conviction that the thoughtless state is always available, every moment, as the backdrop.

When you sleep six to eight hours every night, there are no thoughts. So the thoughtless state is evident during deep sleep. When we are in a thoughtless state in sleep, we forget everything. We forget our name, our profession and even our body. We forget our fatigue as well as all our physical and mental problems. Whatever the intensity of our sufferings, we forget all our difficulties and worries in sleep. That is why everybody wants to get sleep, and we feel restless and unwell if we are unable to get sleep.

On waking up in the morning, the 'I' thought arises and in a fraction of a second the whole fabric of our personalized world is constructed before us in the form of our thoughts – the same 'I', the same name, the same house, the same relatives, the same everything. A moment back, there was nothing and the next moment the world of thoughts emerges. Due to the 'I' thought, the entire world emerges in a flash.

Seeker 2: So there are no thoughts at all while we are asleep?

Sirshree: There can be periods of sleep when thoughts do occur. These thoughts manifest as dreams. A dream appears as real as this waking state to the 'I' thought that presides in the dream. When we wake up, we realise that it was only a dream, only because the reference 'I' thought has changed. But we seldom doubt the authenticity of the waking world; we never question, to whom this world is appearing!

Seeker 3: Can we experience the thoughtless state when we are awake? Even after sitting in meditation for a long period, I am unable to be in that experience. The mind keeps pulling my attention. How can I experience the state of inner stillness?

Sirshree: With consistent practice, you can wakefully experience the thoughtless state, just as you experience blankness during deep sleep. Actually, there is no need to explicitly bring that deep-sleep experience into the waking state, because it is already present right now. The reason you are not able to experience that state is because you have your own concepts and imaginations about it.

You keep comparing what you experience with your imaginations. The mind compares both experiences – waking and deep-sleep. In deep sleep, the feeling of the body disappears; pain and suffering are absent. The mind expects to wakefully experience this same state. When you try to make an effort to wakefully experience this state, the mind might complain: "My head is throbbing and my back is aching. Why can't I experience the blankness devoid of body sensations when I'm awake?" Until the experience of pure being beyond thoughts is truly recognized, it seems very subtle and difficult.

Let us understand this further with the help of an example. Imagine that you are sitting in a room where a soft music is being played. You are asked to listen to the music. But there is a lot of noise in the room, which makes it difficult for you to hear the soft music. You would say, "Stop this noise. I am unable to hear the music because of the noise." But even when everything is silenced, you are still not able to hear the music because you have preconceived notions about the music too. You are trying to listen for the music that is familiar to you, the one that have heard before. If the music that is in your memory is not being played, then you won't recognize or hear the music that is being played. Gradually, once you begin to understand the new sounds, you begin to realize: "This is music too! I was only comparing it with my preconceived ideas. This is different." Now you begin to perceive it. Then you experiment to see whether you are able to hear the music even when there is noise all around. When you get attuned to that music, you will be able to hear it even in the loudness of the surroundings.

Similarly, *when you are able to experience consciousness in the silence of meditation, you will gradually begin to experience it in the noise of the marketplace too.* You will realize that this is what you have experienced even during deep sleep. You realize that this experience of consciousness has always been with you; it never left you. In truth, you are this experience.

But as soon as the mind hears about anything, it immediately assumes and fixes imaginary pictures about it. Initially, the mind will try to draw some imaginary pictures of the experience of consciousness. You may compare it with the blank state of deep sleep. Your mind may also place stipulations on the experience by saying, "It should feel in this particular way, in this part of the body with this intensity etc." But the mind needs to be told that such stipulations are not necessary. These imaginary ideas of the mind are nothing but obstacles that will distract your meditative state.

The sense of conscious presence is always constant. When you sense your presence, you realize that your living presence is the same as it has been since childhood. No change has taken place in your presence. Things may have changed externally, but internally your living presence has always been constant. There is a feeling of continuity through all these years because your presence has not changed within you. Your sense of aliveness is still the same as it was in your childhood. Try to remember what you looked like in your childhood. Many people cannot believe that they looked as they see themselves in their childhood photographs. Yet you do not feel that you have changed. That's because there's one thing in common between your past and present states. You sense that who-you-are-now is the same as who-was-present during childhood. But what is it that is still the same? The sense of presence, the experience of beingness. It is easy to grasp, as it constantly exists. Your height, weight, everything else has changed. Nothing is the same, except your sense of presence. It is this presence that you experience in deep sleep, and which you want to feel even in the waking state. You just need to get rid of your imaginary ideas about it.

So what remains to be done now? Well, nothing. Just sit down and watch the scenes that appear before you. When a scene appears, watch it and when it does not, then experience the presence of consciousness in which the scenes appear and dissolve. It is just as simple.

Seeker 3: Is it possible to abide in this state forever?

Sirshree: Yes it is! You can surely abide in the timeless state of being in and through all your activities, at all times, whether you are awake, dreaming or in deep sleep, regardless of changes in mood, memory, weather, or surroundings. Being in that state is effortless because it is what-you-truly-are. You need to clearly recognize it and develop conviction about it.

So far we talked about the difference between the sense of body and the sense of being. We also looked at the training required to deal with various thoughts, emotions, feelings and body sensations that arise in the body during meditation. Irrespective of these changes, irrespective of the different states of waking, sleep and dreams, the body can still serve as an instrument to experience pure consciousness. This state can be called *Samadhi*. *Samadhi can be attained through consistent practice of meditation. We can stabilize in that state forever.* When we abide in this state, we can be absorbed in our true nature even while the body-mind is engaged in worldly activity.

10

The Path and the Ultimate Goal

Seeker 1: My friend has taken a break from his workplace to practice meditation. I've understood that we do not need to leave productive life to practice meditation. But, isn't meditation a more effective way of transcending action and resting in pure consciousness?

Sirshree: *The practice of meditation has been grossly misunderstood as that of inaction. This is a missing link. Meditation is the state of being absorbed in Self. Meditation is your essential nature. When viewed as the state of being in Self-awareness, meditation has nothing to do with doing or non-doing. It is not an escape from the world. One can be engaged in action while being absorbed in the state of Self-meditation.*

The term, meditation, is also used to refer to the practice that leads to this state, the state of being in Self-awareness. When considered as a practice, meditation is the process of stilling the mind. The mind tends to indulge in thoughts of the world. Incessant thinking becomes a habit. It is a compulsive dis-ease, as it keeps you away from the state of complete ease. The practice of meditation helps you to detach from thoughts that plague your awareness. It raises the awareness of pure consciousness.

In a nutshell, *the daily practice of meditation is a preparation to connect with the world in the right way. It prepares you to abide in the awareness of Self, while being engaged in worldly activity.*

Self-expression is an important aspect of the complete purpose of life. You need to bring the divine qualities of consciousness like love, bliss, peace, creativity, compassion, and patience into expression in worldly life. Meditation helps you to prepare yourself to abide in Self and express these divine qualities.

Seeker 1: Thank you, Sirshree. This helps to clarify that I need not withdraw or take a break from my daily or routine activities to practice meditation. As you said that the practice of meditation prepares one to connect with the world in the right way. Does it also mean that the practice of meditation precedes that of actions?

Sirshree: *Meditation can be viewed as a double-headed arrow. While your focus is directed on the world and its affairs, this very focus on the world serves to illumine the knowing presence. The light of awareness, which illumines everything that is being known, reflects on itself. Awareness becomes aware of itself.*

The more you dwell in the state of meditation on Self, it serves as a thinner to weaken your attachment to the mind's notions, beliefs, and tendencies. The habit of identifying with personality is weakened. You remain absorbed in pure consciousness – the very light in which everything arises and subsides.

Being absorbed in the Self automatically transforms your action. Your actions become increasingly non-personalized, arising from the immaculate standpoint of totality. Actions happen not from the notion of 'doing', but from the essence of 'being'. In this way, meditation translates into inspired action.

However, the converse is also true. The practice of conscious action backed by higher understanding naturally leads the seeker into a meditative state. When actions are performed in the remembrance of the Self the one who-you-truly-are, one rises beyond doing and non-doing. Detached witnessing then gains precedence. While actions happen through the body-mind, the detached witnessing presence becomes increasingly prominent. *Every action is an opportunity, an invitation to honour the divine presence that enlivens it.*

To better understand this in today's technological world, performing actions is like online streaming of a video. You watch the video in real-time as it is being downloaded. Here, you cleanse your mind of past conditioning by encountering it through your interactions with the world.

Meditation is like downloading a media file in offline mode for later viewing. It is practiced by being in the stillness of presence. You cleanse your past conditioning by allowing it to rise into your awareness and watching it as a detached witness.

Thus, the one who delves into the depth of Self-meditation naturally begins to manifest inspired actions arising from the non-personal standpoint of the Self. And the one who acts by abiding in constant remembrance of the Self naturally begins to settle into inner stillness of Self-meditation further leading to the thoughtless state and then to the state of Samadhi.

Seeker 1: This has helped to clear these doubts I had about meditation. I had a question about the state of Samadhi. I have heard of Samadhi only in the context of saints. I have always felt that this is a state only saints can attain.

Sirshree: As we have discussed earlier, Samadhi is the state beyond the three states of waking, dreaming and deep-sleep. You can certainly be in this state with consistent practice of meditation.

Seeker 2: What happens in Samadhi?

Sirshree: In Samadhi, the mind becomes still. *Samadhi is a state of being totally rooted in the present moment. It is the experience where you abide in pure consciousness.* It is stepping into your innate nature that is free from all thoughts, emotions, and bodily sensations. *When one reaches Samadhi, there is a deep knowing that all is one, and that "oneness" is at the essence of who-you-are.*

Seeker 3: I have always been fascinated by this word Samadhi. I have also read that there are different forms of Samadhi. How true is that?

Sirshree: Yes there are different kinds of Samadhi. Let's look at them. The first is Samadhi in deep sleep state. Everyone, without exception, experiences the state of Samadhi while in deep sleep. But you are neither conscious nor aware of the hours that pass. It is only when you wake up in the morning that you are aware that you've slept. *During deep sleep, you lose the sense of body and unawarely exist in the state of Samadhi.* But after getting up in the morning, you again slip into the non-awareness of your true nature by assuming yourself to be the body. As a result, you get completely engrossed in the world and are lost to the experience of Samadhi.

The second is *Savikalpa Samadhi: The simple meaning of savikalpa Samadhi is attaining that state of Samadhi with the help of some supportive means.* These supportive means or techniques could be breath-watching, chanting of a mantra, focusing on the third-eye point between the eyebrows. In Savikalpa Samadhi you become a witness. You begin by watching and discerning the many things around you. You become aware of the sounds falling on your ears, the touch felt by your skin, the smells experienced by your nose, the tastes savored by your tongue. Without getting caught up in these sensations, you continue your practice, your sadhana. Slowly, the witness delves deeper into meditation. You begin to watch the thoughts that are running in your mind, but still persist with the practice. Gradually, the number of thoughts reduces. Thoughts involving your imagination and beliefs are dispelled and the checker and credit-taker thoughts dissolve. By watching and understanding thoughts, the wisdom that such thoughts are serving as a reminder of the witnessor awakens. The witnessing then turns into Self-witnessing. The world and body-mind serve as pretexts to recognize and experience the Self.

What follows is the state of Nirvikalpa Samadhi. In this state, there is no need for any supportive means. Let me give you an example that will help you understand this state easily. You use a boat to help cross a river. Once you have reached the opposite side of the river, the boat is no longer required for your onward journey. What do you do after that? You abandon the boat. Similarly all such means are no longer required once you have attained the state of Self-witnessing. Only the experience of beingness remains.

In this state you experientially know who-you-truly-are. When you arrive in this state consciously, you attain absolute conviction of your true nature. You realize that you are beyond time and space, beyond body, mind and intellect.

Finally, there comes the state of Sahaj Samadhi. This is a state in which you can naturally abide in the timeless state of being in and through all our activities, at all times, whether you are awake, dreaming or in deep sleep, regardless of changes in mood, memory, weather, or surroundings. It becomes effortless for you to be in that state. *You stabilize in that state forever. You abide in constant remembrance of who-you-truly-are at all times, even while the body-mind is engaged in worldly activity.*

Being stabilized in the experience of the Self, we witness how our body functions in various situations. The qualities of the Self – such as love, joy, peace, compassion, patience, creativity and courage – are then expressed through our body. The body-mind becomes an instrument for the highest expression of the Self. Once this state is reached, you experientially realize the ultimate purpose of being embodied on Earth, leading to the eternal state..

So just as a mirror serves as a medium to see yourself, your body serves as a mirror to know your true nature. You witness the world of senses only to know the sense of being. You neither get deluded by the experiences of the body nor by the world of the senses. You always have the conviction that whatever is happening is with the body and not with you. You are then stabilized in the conviction that you are not the body; you are the sense of being, the sense of presence, pure consciousness which is eternal.

Seeker 1: Sirshree, you spoke about the eternal state which is the ultimate purpose of being embodied on Earth. What is that state?

Sirshree: It is called the *Turiyateet* state. *Turiya means the 'fourth' – it represents the state of Samadhi beyond the three states of waking, dreaming and deep-sleep. "Turiyateet" is beyond Turiya – beyond the* *fourth, where the state of Samadhi is transcended. This is the state of Self-in-rest.* This is the ultimate goal of meditation.

In this transcended state, the 'I' ceases to exist and so does all knowledge. It transcends both knowledge and ignorance. What remains is just 'am'… 'amness'… 'isness'. Here, there are no words, just absolute silence, which is beyond both sound and silence. It is the original state of the Self in which thoughts arise and fade away into nothingness; just as waves arise from the ocean and die into its vast expanse. *This state of Self-in-rest is the ever-present Source, the background, the substratum of everything that is manifest. It is pure nothingness with the potential of everything.*

It might seem difficult to comprehend at this stage as it is beyond the confines of the human intellect to know the state that can be only experienced. When you religiously practice meditation, it will surely culminate here. This is the whole and sole purpose of life.

You can send your opinion or feedback on this book to :

Tej Gyan Foundation, Pimpri Colony, P. O. Box 25, Pimpri, Pune – 411017 (Maharashtra), INDIA
email : mail@tejgyan.com

About Sirshree

Sirshree's spiritual quest which began during his childhood, led him on a journey through various schools of thought and meditation practices. His overpowering desire to attain the truth made him relinquish his teaching job. After a long period of contemplation, his spiritual quest culminated in the attainment of the ultimate truth. Sirshree says, **"All paths that lead to the truth begin differently, but end in the same way—with understanding. Understanding is the whole thing. Listening to this understanding is enough to attain the truth."**

Sirshree is the author of several spiritual books. His books have been translated in more than 10 languages and published by leading publishers such as Penguin and Hay House. He is the founder of Tej Gyan Foundation, a not-for-profit organization committed to raising mass consciousness by spreading "Happy Thoughts" with branches in the United States, India, Europe and Asia-Pacific. Sirshree's retreats have transformed the lives of thousands and his teachings have inspired various social initiatives for raising global consciousness.

His works include more than 100 books and 3000 discourses. Various luminaries and celebrities such as His Holiness the Dalai Lama, publishers Mr. Reid Tracy and Ms. Tami Simon and yoga master Dr. B. K. S Iyengar have released Sirshree's books and lauded his work. 'The Source' book series, authored by Sirshree, has sold more than 10 million copies in 5 years. His book *The Warrior's Mirror*, published by Penguin, was featured in the Limca Book of Records for being released on the same day in 11 languages.

Tejgyan... The Road Ahead

What is Tejgyan?

Tejgyan is the existential wisdom of the ultimate truth, which is beyond duality. In today's world, there are people who feel disharmony and are desperately trying to achieve balance in an unpredictable life. Tejgyan helps them in harmonizing with their true nature, the Self, thereby restoring balance in all aspects of their life.

And then there are those who are successful but feel a sense of emptiness or void within. Tejgyan provides them fulfillment and helps them to embark on a journey towards self-realization. There are others who feel lost and are seeking the meaning of life. Tejgyan helps them to realize the true purpose of human life.

All this is possible with Tejgyan due to a very simple reason. The experience of the ultimate truth is always available. The direct experience of this truth is possible provided the right method is known. Tejgyan is that method, that understanding. At Tej Gyan Foundation, Sirshree imparts this understanding through a System for Wisdom – a series of retreats that guides participants step by step

Magic of Ultimate Awakening Retreat

Magic of Ultimate Awakening is the flagship self-realization retreat offered by Tej Gyan Foundation The retreat is conducted in two languages – Hindi and English. The teachings of the retreat are non-denominational (secular).

About Tej Gyan Foundation

Tej Gyan Foundation (TGF) was established with the mission of creating a highly evolved society through all-round self development of every individual that transforms all the facets of his/her life. It is a non-profit organization founded on the teachings of Sirshree. The foundation has received the ISO certification (ISO 9001:2015) for its system of imparting wisdom. It has centres all across India as well as in other countries. The motto of Tej Gyan Foundation is 'Happy Thoughts'.

TGF is creating a highly evolved society through:

- Tejgyan Programs (Retreats, Courses, Television and Radio Programs, Podcasts)

- Tejgyan Products (Books, Tapes, Audio/Video CDs)

- Tejgyan Projects (Value Education, Women Empowerment, Peace Initiatives)

TGF undertakes projects to elevate the level of consciousness among students, youth, women, senior citizens, teachers, doctors, leaders, organizations, police force, prisoners, etc.

MaNaN Ashram

Survey No. 43, Sanas Nagar, Nandoshi gaon,Kirkatwadi Phata, Sinhagad Road, Dist. Pune 411024, Maharashtra, India.

Books can be delivered at your doorstep by registered post or courier. You can request for the same through postal money order or pay by VPP. Please send the money order to either of the following two addresses:

. WOW Publishings Pvt. Ltd

1. Registered Office: E-4, Vaibhav Nagar, Near Tapovan Mandir, Pimpri, Pune 411017.

2. Post Box No. 36, Pimpri Colony Post Office, Pimpri, , Pune 411017

Phone No. : 9011013210 / 9623457873

You can also order your copy at the online store:
www.gethappythoughts.org

*Free Shipping plus 10% Discount on purchases above Rs. 300/-.

For further details contact:

Tejgyan Global Foundation

Registered Office:
Happy Thoughts Building, Vikrant Complex, Near Tapovan Mandir, Pimpri, Pune 411017, Maharashtra, India.
Contact No: 020-27411240, 27412576
Email: mail@tejgyan.com

MaNaN Ashram:
Survey No. 43, Sanas Nagar, Nandoshi gaon, Kirkatwadi Phata, Sinhagad Road, Tal. Haveli, Dist. Pune 411024, Maharashtra, India.
Contact No: 992100 8060.

Hyderabad: 9885558100, **Bangalore:** 9880412588,

Delhi: 9891059875, **Nashik:** 9326967980, **Mumbai:** 9373440985

For accessing our unique 'System for Wisdom' from self-help to self-realization, please follow us on:

	Website	www.tejgyan.org
YouTube	Video Channel	www.youtube.com/tejgyan For Q&A videos: http://goo.gl/YA81DQ
facebook	Social networking	www.facebook.com/tejgyan
twitter	Social networking	www.twitter.com/sirshree
	Internet Radio	http://www.tejgyan.org/internetradio.aspx

Online Shopping
www.gethappythoughts.org

Pray for World Peace along with thousands of others at 09:09 a.m. and p.m. every day